GET YOUR SHELL ON

adapted by Natalie Shaw

Ready-to-Read

JEZ
SHAW

Simon Spotlight

New York   London   Toronto   Sydney   New Delhi

SIMON SPOTLIGHT

An imprint of Simon & Schuster Children's Publishing Division
1230 Avenue of the Americas, New York, New York 10020
DreamWorks Turbo © 2013 DreamWorks Animation L.L.C.
All rights reserved, including the right of reproduction in whole or in part in any form.
SIMON SPOTLIGHT, READY-TO-READ, and colophon are registered trademarks of Simon & Schuster, Inc.
For information about special discounts for bulk purchases, please contact Simon & Schuster
Special Sales at 1-866-506-1949 or business@simonandschuster.com.
Manufactured in the United States of America 0413 LAK
First Edition
10 9 8 7 6 5 4 3 2 1
ISBN 978-1-4424-8474-0 (pbk)
ISBN 978-1-4424-8475-7 (hc)
ISBN 978-1-4424-8476-4 (eBook)

Turbo is a little snail
with a big dream.
He wants to race!

Turbo even has a racecourse!
But snails are pretty slow.

One day Turbo changes.
He is not slow anymore.
He is speedy.
His eyes light up
like headlights!

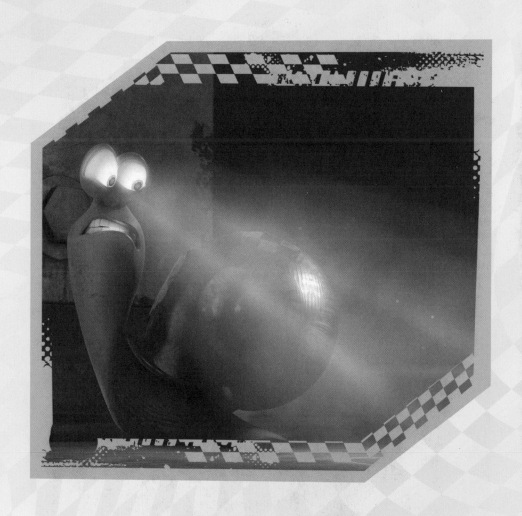

Turbo goes on an adventure
with his brother, Chet.
They end up at a
shopping center.

Other snails are there too.
They are racing snails!

Whiplash is the leader
of the racing snail crew.
Whiplash looks tough,
but he is nice.

Skidmark is blue.
When he moves,
he makes a screeching sound!

Burn has a red shell.
Flames fly behind her
when she races.

Smoove Move looks cool.
He wears fuzzy dice
around his neck.

White Shadow is big.
He says he is so fast that
all you see is his shadow!

Now it is time to race!

White Shadow
jumps onto a board.
He makes the snails
fly into the air!

The snails use cool moves
to race down a cable.
They slide toward the
finish line!

Smoove Move slides down
the cable on a stick!

Turbo thinks the snails
are awesome!
Then he shows them
what he can do!

Whiplash and his crew
join Team Turbo!

Then Turbo goes to race
real cars at the Indy 500!

For the big race,
Turbo gets a cool
new blue shell.

Turbo is a fast snail.
But is he fast enough
to win?

The race is on!
Turbo and the race cars
drive lap after lap.

Turbo goes
under a car, up a wall,
and into the lead.

Turbo wins the race
by a shell!
Go, Team Turbo!